CHARLOTTE BAKEMAN HAS HER SAY

Mary E. Finger

Charlotte Bakeman
Has Her Say

ILLUSTRATED BY

Kimberly Rose Batti

LITTLE PEAR PRESS
SEEKONK, MA

Little Pear Press
Seekonk, MA 02771
www.littlepearpress.com
© 2007 by Mary E. Finger
Cover and illustrations © 2007 Kimberly Rose Batti
Design by Christina Gruppuso
Printed in the USA
ISBN: 0-9746-9112-7
ISBN 13: 978-0-9746-9112-1
Library of Congress Control Number: 2007930758

ACKNOWLEDGEMENTS

I want to thank Kathryn Green, Martha Manno, and Elizabeth Stabler, members of my writing group, for patient and sensitive help over the years. Thanks also to Renelle L'Huillier McLaughlin for help with matters French Canadian. And finally I would like to express extra gratitude to Martha Manno, a superb editor.

To Amy, Max, Katie, Wendall and Anna

BIG TROUBLE IN THE SCHOOL YARD

I was all alone, leaning against the trunk of the big maple in the Green Glen School yard waiting for my best friend Francie. She couldn't come out for recess until she had "a little talk" with our teacher, Miss Harris.

It wasn't that I especially liked being alone, but at least, when I was under the tree, people didn't notice me so much.

Except for Leona. There she was, walking toward me. "Leona the moaner," Francie calls her because she's always begging for attention. She lives in West Glen. Most of the fathers there work in the mill, and most of the families are French Canadian. "Canucks," some of the kids call them when they're being mean or making fun of them.

I slid around the trunk of the maple and started towards the girls' door. Hurry up, Francie. I tried to push my thoughts through the door on the girls' side, up the wide staircase, down the hall that smelled of floor oil and into the sixth grade room. Hurry up. Save me from Leona.

Then right away I got into an even worse mess. I was face to face with Miriam and Alice. The Terrible

Twosome, Francie and I called them—because they liked to get together and pick on other kids. They were always saying mean things and thinking of ways to make the rest of us feel bad. And they were the tallest girls in the class, too.

Francie wouldn't have been afraid of them. She wasn't afraid of anything. In fact, that's why she was having a "little talk" with Miss Harris. It was about interrupting people. Francie gets excited when the class is discussing something and she bursts out with what she wants to say before the other person has finished.

Today at current-events time when Chuckie was telling about the Lindbergh baby being kidnapped, Francie called out, "Bruno Richard Hauptmann—that's who they think did it!"

"I was just going to say that," grumbled Chuckie.

I know it's rude to interrupt people, but actually I envy Francie because I'm just the opposite. I wait too long, and by the time I'm ready to get into the conversation everyone's talking about something else. I wish I could speak out quickly, but I'm a shy person. It's just the way I am. I guess it's why I liked standing more or less out of sight under the big maple.

It was a good place, anyway, until Leona found me. And now Miriam and Alice began to make fun of me.

"Look, there's little Miss Stuck-up," Miriam sang out in her prissy voice. "Thinks she's so great 'cause she won the essay contest." Miriam had entered the contest, too, and I heard her saying that the prize should have gone to someone who wrote about Martin Green, the man our town was named for. Guess what? Miriam's essay was about Martin Green.

"Yeah, thinks she's so great," Alice echoed. "Her father probably wrote it for her."

"He did not!" Just because my father wrote articles for the *Green Glen Times* didn't mean he wrote my essay. All he did was suggest that I find out about the old brickyard. I did all the research myself and I wrote the essay myself. But even if I could get the words out to explain to Miriam and Alice, I knew they wouldn't listen.

"My mother said no sixth grader would know all those big words you used." Miriam continued the attack in her "better-than-you" voice.

"Yeah, that's right," said Alice pushing her big, lopsided mouth right in front of my face.

Other girls were coming up behind them. I wished Francie would come. I was getting hot and sweaty. I wished I was someplace else—*any* place!

Behind me was an opening where we'd pulled back the chain-link fence to make a shortcut to the street. Before I even thought about it, I bolted. Through the fence and across the street, up the Newtons' driveway, across their yard, and on out back through their vegetable garden. I moved like the wind.

The corn stalks at the end of the garden rustled like paper when I brushed against them. Then I heard a low growl. The Newtons' bull terrier, snarling and showing his teeth, hurled himself toward me. I felt prickles coming on the back of my neck. I put on extra speed and went over the stone wall so fast that I scraped my knee.

When I turned around to get a look at the dog, I saw somebody following me. Then I tripped on a tree root and fell flat on my face on the pine needles.

THE RUNAWAYS

Charlotte, help me."

Wouldn't you know?—it was Leona running through the garden toward me. I scrambled to my feet and saw the dog jump at her. She put her arms up in the air and twisted back and forth, trying to get away from the snarling bull terrier who kept leaping and snapping at her. I shouted to her to come over the wall. When she was close enough, I caught her arm and yanked her over.

"Run!" I yelled.

"I can't."

"You have to."

I had enough trouble without having dumb old Leona to take care of. I jerked her to her feet, and we ran hand in hand on a path through the tall pine trees until we had to stop because we were both out of breath.

The dog hadn't come over the wall, thank goodness. He let out a few half-hearted barks. He seemed to say that the woods were not his responsibility, but we had better stay out of his field.

"Why did you follow me?"

"I dunno." Leona shrugged her shoulders. "Guess I was scared of Miriam and Alice, too."

"I wasn't scared."

"Then why'd you run?"

"I just didn't want to talk to them."

"I call that being scared."

Darn Leona. Of course I was scared, but I didn't want to admit it. Being shy makes you scared of lots of things and it also makes you afraid to admit it. Darn, darn Leona, I didn't want to talk to her either. But here she was, grabbing at my sweater and whimpering.

"Charlotte, are we lost? I don't like these woods."

"Don't be silly," I said. I wasn't afraid of the woods the way Leona was, but to tell the truth, you might say we were a little lost, because I hadn't ever been here before. We were on a path, but it wasn't well tramped like the paths in Cunningham's woods, where Francie and I usually played.

The pine needles on the ground were the same, though. They glowed in the sunshine like a copper-colored carpet. And overhead was the same soft sighing sound as the wind moved through the tops of the pine trees. Here and there were splashes of yellow and red where the maple leaves were beginning to change to their fall colors in the midst of the pines and hemlocks, which kept their green year round. It was quiet and lovely—until suddenly there was an explosion, as if an engine had backfired in the bushes right in front of us. Dry leaves and pine needles flew all around, and my heart pounded in my chest.

IN THE WOODS

Leona grabbed me again, and this time I didn't blame her. My heart was thumping, and I was frightened, too—for a minute. Then I saw a large bird flying away from us, low over the underbrush at first and then up into the air with a noisy whir of wings, and soon out of sight. I laughed.

"Partridge," I told her. "It's happened to me before. They wait until you're almost on top of them, then they crash out of the bushes. Surprises you every time."

"I didn't know there was stuff like that out here," Leona's voice was shaky, and I thought she might start to cry. "Big birds that could knock you down. I bet there are wild animals, too. Bears and tigers and things like that." She sounded frantic and asked once more, "Are you sure we're not lost?"

I told her we were in Brewster's Woods. Actually I wasn't sure of that, but I wasn't going to let on to Leona. The last thing I needed was for her to get into any more of a panic. So I tried to sound calm, even though I didn't feel that way.

When I thought about being calm instead of worrying and being afraid all the time, it reminded me of The March of Time newsreel I saw at the movies one Saturday afternoon. President Roosevelt was making a speech, and in the part they showed on the screen he said, "We have nothing to fear, but fear itself." I had thought about that a lot—"nothing to fear, but fear itself." He was talking about the whole country, of course, needing to stop being afraid of the Depression and to begin to work our way out of it. Even though I knew my dad didn't like Roosevelt and his ideas, I thought perhaps this idea of his might have something to do with me, too. I wondered if "fear itself" was what made me shy.

"Brewster's Woods are next to Cunningham's," I told her. I was pretty sure of that. I tried to talk like Miss Harris did when she was explaining something. "Brewster's Woods are next to Cunningham's," I repeated, maybe hoping to convince myself, too, "and when we get to Cunningham's, we'll be okay. Francie and I have a hideaway there."

I didn't really want to take Leona to the Hideaway, but I needed to be someplace familiar so I could get us out of the woods, and I surely wasn't going back by the Newtons' dog.

The Hideaway was a place Francie and I had fixed for ourselves where there was a high rock ledge, a foot or two taller than we were. It was a wonderful spot close to the brook and it usually took us about ten minutes to get to it on the path which started in the woods across the road from my house at the end of Spring Street. That's the way I'd always gone to it before, and I thought I'd find it from this direction, too. But I wasn't sure.

When Francie and I first decided on the Hideaway, we searched all over the woods for long sticks, dragged them back and put them lean-to style against the ledge. This was what we called our Hideaway, but the only really secret part was a crevice in the ledge. A couple of stiff, prickly juniper bushes, with light blue wrinkly berries, hid the secret place from sight. When Francie and I pulled the bushes back and crawled into the split in the rock behind them, no one could see us hiding there. I decided I wasn't going to show that part to Leona.

We kept walking. The sun was high overhead, and I thought it was probably about noontime. We'd left the school at morning recess and had been walking quite a while, longer, I think, than it took me to walk to school on the sidewalk on Spring Street. The path we were fol-

lowing, if I was calculating right, would be roughly parallel to Spring Street. So if I was right, we should get to the Hideaway soon. But, of course, it was slower walking in the woods, and there was also the chance that we might be walking the wrong way.

Leona was acting like a real baby. She fussed about bugs and being hungry and said she was sure we were lost. I was worried, too. If we were going in the wrong direction, we might even have to spend the night out here. That was scary.

Running away from that dumb school yard had felt wonderful at the time. I was scared, and I'd done it quick, without thinking. I hardly ever do things without thinking. But now I didn't feel so wonderful. I hated Miriam and Alice. This was all their fault. And it was Leona's fault, too. If she hadn't started to pester me, I wouldn't have had to run away. I knew that wasn't really fair, but it made me feel better to be mad at her, too.

"I'm hungry," Leona said for about the fifteenth time.

Francie and I had crackers at the Hideaway, but even if we got there, I wasn't going to tell Leona about them because they were hidden in the secret part. They were in our treasure box. The treasure box was really an old steel file box my father gave me when he was cleaning out his office at work. It was good for keeping things dry in the woods. Francie and I kept books in it, too, wrapped in a pouch which had once held Mrs. Cunningham's raincoat.

I wondered whether the narrow path we were on had been made by people or by animals. I didn't have to wonder long, because the path soon ended at a brook. It was one which a raccoon or some other animal used to get to the water.

"How are we going to get to the other side?" Leona whined.

"We don't have to. We'll follow the brook and it will take us to Cunningham's Woods."

I didn't really know this, but I hoped it was the same brook. It was just about as wide. Anyway, I knew about following a brook. Once in the *Manchester Union* I saw a picture of a boy who was separated from his family on Mount Washington and had found his way to the state road by following a brook downstream. He was younger than me, and the picture showed him standing next to a police officer who praised him for knowing that going downstream beside the brook would bring him down off the mountain after a while.

We walked along beside the brook and watched it sometimes spreading out in quiet pools, other times bubbling over a bed of stones. Leona didn't seem so scared any more. She was even beginning to relax and enjoy herself.

"I wish I had my sketch pad," she said. Leona liked to draw, and she practically always had a sketch pad with her. I realized that she was seeing lots of things that probably were new and different for her and that she would like to get them down on paper. I had often wished I could draw as fast and as well as she could.

We tossed sticks and leaves into the brook and watched to see which one got down a certain stretch of water first, sort of like Christopher Robin and Winnie the Pooh playing Pooh Sticks. It would have been fun to just stay there watching the sticks and leaves and water bugs, and all the other interesting things floating by, but I said we had to keep going because I was afraid of getting caught in the woods overnight. The sun was no longer directly overhead, and my stomach told me that it was well after lunchtime.

After walking beside the brook for quite a while longer, we came to a stone wall. Beyond it I thought I could see a mossy roof, like the one on the Cunningham's springhouse. I climbed up on the wall, looked over, and let out a big, "Hurray!"

"Why hurray?"

"Because I can see the Cunningham's springhouse. Now I know exactly where we are."

"I thought you knew before."

"I did, sort of—but not exactly. Now I know exactly."

"Then why are you crying?"

"I'm not really crying," I said, even though tears were running down my face. Actually I was laughing a little, too. It seemed funny to be laughing and crying at the same time, but I was relieved to know we weren't lost.

"I think you're acting weird," Leona said.

"Never mind. Come on."

Soon we were on a little rise where we could see the Hideaway.

"Darn those boys," I said.

"What boys?"

"Francie's brother and his friend Leo. Every so often they mess up our place. Francie and I always put things back the way we like them."

They had hung an old blanket at the side of the lean-to—maybe they were trying to make their own hiding place.

Then I saw something much worse. A man sitting in the afternoon sun with his back to the ledge, reading a newspaper. Who was he? And what was he doing here? We had to get away. Even Francie would say it was okay to run away from a stranger.

I was a few steps ahead of Leona. I turned around and put my finger to my lips, then started to walk Indian style—that was a way we practiced walking in the woods, going on tiptoe and not stepping on any twigs, not making any noise.

But of course Leona didn't catch on.

"What's the matter?" she asked, her voice loud and clear.

The man heard her, turned around, and looked straight at us.

4

THE TRAMP

W ell, hello." The man raised his voice at the end of
the "hello" and sounded surprised. His face was
tanned, and he had dark brown curly hair and
dark brown eyes. It was the same tramp who came to our
house yesterday asking for food.

Yesterday I watched from behind the curtains of the
dining-room window while he sat on the side porch eat-
ing the soup and bread my mother gave him. His pants
were greasy, and the sole of one shoe was taped to the
upper part with dirty adhesive tape. He had to go around
asking people for food because he didn't have a job.

Lots of men were losing their jobs because of the
Depression. I didn't know exactly what the Depression
was, except that grown-ups talked about it a lot, and
it was bad because nobody had enough money. Every
so often there was a story in the newspaper or on the
radio about businessmen in New York or Chicago who
committed suicide by jumping from a high building into
the street. The men who did this were so worried about
their money problems that killing themselves seemed to
be the only answer. And in the Sunday newspaper there
were often pictures of Hoovervilles, named for President
Hoover because the people living there blamed him for

their troubles. Hoovervilles were shantytowns where poor people lived in tents or in shacks made out of packing boxes, old railroad cars or anything else they could find. The people in the pictures looked raggedy and miserable, and I used to spend hours looking at them, especially at the children, and wondering how anybody could stand living there and why anybody had to live like that and why they couldn't find better places to live. But there was no Hooverville in Green Glen, thank goodness, and here the Depression just seemed to mean that there were a few tramps wandering around looking for handouts and everyone else worrying about money and losing their jobs.

Jimmy Roberts' father used to work in Simon's real-estate office, but he lost his job and now he drove a rickety old truck around town collecting rubbish, and Jimmy pretended he didn't see him when the truck rattled by the school. Monica Lamb's father had just been laid off. I wondered if he was going to be a tramp. What if my father lost his job as editor of the *Green Glen Times*? Would he have to go around to people's back doors asking for food? What would happen to Mother and me? Would I have to go to an orphanage? I worried about these things.

Today the tramp had added a gray jacket to his outfit, the kind which goes with a suit men wear to work. It looked strange with the greasy pants, but I was glad he had something warmer for the cool fall weather.

"Didn't expect company, I didn't," he said. "You two, what're you doing out here, anyway?" he asked.

I wanted to say, "What are you doing here?" But of course I didn't, because of being shy about talking to grown-ups.

Leona couldn't keep quiet, though. "We ran away from school," she said.

"You ran away from school! Mon der," he said, or something that sounded like that. "How come?"

She told him about Miriam and Alice.

The tramp nodded. "Sound like real meanies, them two," he said.

"And a dog tried to bite me." Leona was telling the tramp everything. "And there was this big bird—a duck, I think."

"A partridge," I said and explained what had happened. He laughed when I told him how much it had surprised us.

"Same thing happens to me when I'm hunting. Takes a lot to shake me up, it does. But them partridges, they can do it every time." He chuckled and waved his hands up in the air. "Whoosh! Up they go right in front of you and set your heart to pounding."

I noticed a rolled-up blanket on the ground near him, and beside that a rumpled paper bag. He picked it up and said, "Here, have a doughnut. I bet you're hungry."

"Gee, thanks. We're starving," Leona said helping herself to a sugar doughnut. I just shook my head. I wanted one, too, but I didn't want to take his food away from him. There would be food for me at home, and perhaps this was all he had.

"Worried about taking my food?" He seemed to read my mind. "It's okay. Fellow at the bakery give me this whole bag of day-old ones." He thrust it at me. "More than I can eat."

There *were* a lot of doughnuts in the bag. I picked one covered with cinnamon and sat down on a flat rock to eat it.

He bit into a jelly doughnut. "Now," he said, "tell me how you two got way out here in the woods."

"We followed the brook," Leona told him. "Charlotte knows all about the woods, and she said that's what we should do."

"Smart girl."

I explained how I had been trying to get to the Hideaway. I was beginning to feel better about talking to the tramp. It was easier than with most grown-ups because he wasn't just being polite. He really seemed to care about what Leona and I had to say.

"This is your hideaway—yes?" the tramp asked. "Not much of a hideaway. Right out in the open."

I wasn't going to tell him about the secret hiding place,

so I said, "We just call it that. Francie and I. She's my best friend."

"So your name's Francine?" he asked Leona.

"No," Leona giggled. "Not Francine, Francie. And that's not me. I'm Leona, Leona Fontaine."

"And that's French. N'est-ce pas?"

"Oui," Leona said quickly. "Je suis Francaise."

"Moi, aussi. Je m'appelle Armand. Armand Boudreau."

I felt funny when I didn't know what they were saying. I only knew English. I was glad when Leona noticed.

"I told him I'm French, and he told me his name is Armand Boudreau," she explained. I could see she liked knowing something I didn't, because in school I'm smarter than she is.

"Let's teach Charlotte some French, eh, Leona?" the tramp said.

Then he said something to me that sounded like *sa va*. "I'm asking you, "How are things?" he said. "Tell her how to answer, Leona."

"*Ça va*."

"It sounds the same to me," I said, "except not a question."

"That's right," he said. "That's the way we do it. Leona said 'Everything's okay.'"

Then he had me try it a few times. I wasn't sure I wanted to learn their kind of French. My mother had told me that when I study French in high school, it'll be different from what the kids in West Glen speak, because theirs is Canadian French, and I would learn Parisian French like they speak in France.

5

TROUBLE AGAIN

The tramp leaned back against the ledge. His eyes were closed, and the sun shone on his face. It was peaceful in the woods, and the slanting rays of sun felt good. I ate my doughnut and listened to the chatter of the brook. And Leona kept still, too, for a change.

After a few minutes the tramp opened his eyes and said, "About these two, Miriam and Alice. Did ya ever think of sassing them right back?"

"No. Well, I mean I've *thought* of it, but I've never done it." I brushed the last of the cinnamon and sugar off my hands, and a whole troop of little ants appeared to carry it away.

"You need to be ready for 'em the next time," he said. "Figure it out ahead of time. What you're gonna say. How you're gonna say it. Practice it out loud. Say it just as strong and mean as they do."

"That's what Francie's always telling me. She says I have to practice not being shy."

I didn't like talking about being shy, but with the tramp it was different. I felt as if I could say whatever I wanted.

Then Leona butted in with a question, "How long have you been a tramp?" she asked him.

"Holy moly, a tramp! Me, I don't think of myself that way. How long since I took to the road? About a month ago—when I got laid off from the mill. The Gurney Mill over in Manton. Most everybody in Manton works there."

"I know where you mean," I told him. Sometimes when my family went swimming at Sunshine Lake, we drove by the big brick mill buildings along the side of the river. There were lots of windows, and I always tried to see the people working inside. When the windows were open, you could hear the machinery clanging and banging. I wondered what it would be like to be cooped up indoors all day with those noisy machines.

"That's when I moved out from my brother's place. They didn't have enough food for their kids, let alone me. Been roaming around through Manton, Green Glen and Oakton ever since. You know those advertisements they

have about the Monadnock Region, beauty spot of southern New Hampshire?" We nodded, and he gave a big sigh. "Well, it's a lot more beautiful if you've got a place to live and enough to eat." He grinned at us. "Heck, I'm doing a lot of blabbing. Haven't had anyone to talk to for a couple days. And you're good listeners, you two are."

I felt sorry he'd lost his job, but I didn't know how to say so. So all I said was, "Uh, huh."

"My dad worries that he'll get laid off," Leona told him. "He works in the blanket factory in West Glen."

"That's where they made a lot of the blankets for the soldiers during the war," I said. "My Uncle Fred found a West Glen label on his blanket when he was fighting in France."

"Really?" the tramp asked. "Our mill in Manton is a cotton mill."

He threw a stone into the brook. He threw it hard, as if he was angry, and it made a big splash. "It's tough," he said. "I was going fishing and bringing home what I could catch. But the fish weren't biting very good. I'd a gone for a deer, even though it wasn't deer season, but I sold my gun when I got laid off. Had to have some money. So, you see, that's why I lit out and gave them one less mouth—"

I didn't hear any more because I had spotted Alan coming round the bend by the crooked pine tree. He was one of the hired men at Mr. Cunningham's chicken farm.

"Here comes Alan. You talk to him," I blurted out. I grabbed Leona with one hand, pulled back the juniper bushes with the other, and dragged her into the secret hiding place. We crouched down in there. Leona looked like she might cry, but thank goodness she kept quiet.

I was pretty nervous, too. Probably the tramp would tell Alan where we were, and we'd be in a heap of trouble, especially me.

"Hey, where'd you come from?" I heard Alan ask.

"From Manton way. Just bumming around."

"Well, you better bum your way right out of here. Mr. Cunningham don't want no tramps hanging around his woods."

I wished Alan wouldn't be so mean. It made me feel bad for the tramp. I didn't like Alan. He was always teasing me—calling the bones in my back "angel wings" when I wore my halter top—and asking if the cat had got my tongue. It would be worse than ever if he discovered I'd hidden from him.

"Seen a couple girls around here?" he asked.

Leona was grabbing me and digging her fingernails into my arm so hard it hurt. Please, please, don't tell on us, I thought to myself—and held my breath.

∼✤ 6 ✤∼

SAVED BY ARMAND BOUDREAU

Therewere a couple girls here a while ago. A skinny one. Straight brown hair, blue eyes. And a dark haired one."

"Yeah, that's them. Charlotte Bakeman and some kid from West Glen. Ran away from the school yard. Everyone's worried about them. The boss told me and Butch—he's the other hired man—to stop work and help look for 'em."

Eek! This was awful. Now everyone in town would know that I had run away. Everyone would be talking about me. I would hate it! I wished I could stay in the hiding place for the rest of my life and never have to face anybody from Green Glen again.

"That so?" said the tramp. "They were here a while ago, but they disappeared. Dunno where they went."

Whew! Thank goodness. I loved the tramp. I was so happy I even hugged Leona.

"You better not be here when I come back," I heard Alan say with a sort of a snarl. When I was sure he was out of sight, Leona and I crept out of the hiding place.

"Thanks a lot," I said, coming up behind the tramp. "Thanks an awful lot."

He turned. "Listen, you two, I didn't know what to say. You disappeared real quick. Where did you go?"

I pulled back the stiff, prickly branches of the juniper bush so he could see the entrance to the secret hiding place.

"It's a place where Francie and I hide from the boys when they come out here pestering us. Except for Francie and me—and now Leona—you're the only other person who knows about it." He seemed like the kind of grown-up you could trust.

For the second time, I felt as if he read my mind. "I'll keep your secret," he said, "but you two, it's getting late. You'd better get home before your mothers start worrying."

"Will you be here tomorrow?" I asked him.

He shook his head. "No, I'll have to clear out after the way that guy talked. I know a troublemaker when I see one."

7

GOING FISHING

I didn't want to go to school the next day. Usually I like to go to school, and I especially like sixth grade with Miss Harris. But today everyone would know that I had run away, and they might laugh at me or tease me about being a fraidy cat. I tried to convince Mother that I might be coming down with a cold, but she made me get up and eat my breakfast. I could tell that she knew what was bothering me because when she shooed me out the door, she said, "Just pretend you don't care. Pretend it's like any other day."

Pretend it's like any other day? That was like the tramp telling me to face up to Miriam and Alice, or Francie saying I shouldn't be shy. Sometimes I feel as if nobody understands me, and they all want to make me different from the way I am.

Francie was waiting in front of her house for me, and we walked to school together the way we always do, first past Baxter's farm and the vegetable stand, which was empty this early in the morning, and on down Spring Street to the bottom of the hill, then crossing over to go up School Street. There was plenty of time to tell Francie about the tramp.

"Wow! My dad said at supper last night that Alan had

chased a tramp out of the woods. But, gee whilikers, I didn't know you'd been talking to him."

I told her about hiding when Alan came—and about Leona.

"Wish it had been me instead of Leona. And now she knows about the Hideaway, too." Francie made a face.

"And so does the tramp."

The wind was making little mounds of red and gold and tan leaves in some places and scattering them about in others. Francie kicked a clump of leaves off the sidewalk into the street. Then she turned to me.

"So, why did you run away?" she asked.

I told her about Miriam and Alice picking on me.

"Miriam and Alice. Oof." Francie let her breath out in a big puff. "Those monsters! How mean can they get?" She stomped on a pile of leaves. "I'd have knocked their heads together," she said fiercely.

I had to laugh at the idea of Francie, who was a lot shorter than either Miriam or Alice, reaching up to knock their heads together. But I knew Francie would have done something brave, and not run off, the way I did.

She must have been thinking the same thing because she said, "You've got to learn to stick up for yourself, Charlotte. You can't be so scared all the time."

"It's just the way I am. I can't help it."

"It's not just the way you are. Think of your grandmother. Her name is Charlotte Bakeman, too—right?"

"Yes," I said softly because I knew what was coming. Francie was going to remind me that Grandma Bakeman was a strong lady, always polite, but never afraid to come right out with the truth. In fact, she had a reputation for being outspoken, which I think embarrassed my parents sometimes. I had seen a picture of her marching with the suffragettes back before women got the vote. I was proud of her, and I wished I could be like her, but I seemed to be different. Speaking up was natural for her. For me, it would take a lot of effort.

We got to school just in time to line up and file in. I was relieved that I didn't have to answer anybody's questions about what happened yesterday. Miss Harris gave me a sort of extra welcoming smile, but didn't say anything about running away. I loved her for that. Later at recess, some of the kids wanted to know where I'd gone, but nobody really teased me, not even Miriam and Alice, who were busy trying out a new jump rope Alice's aunt had given her.

The day went by pretty much like any other until Francie and I stopped on the way home from school at Mr. Baxter's vegetable stand, which now had a good supply of corn, green beans, pumpkins and squash, as well as five different kinds of apples. Mr. Baxter kept the self-service table in front of his house as a convenience for

the neighbors, and Francie and I stopped almost every day to see what there was. Mr. Baxter's stand seemed extra special to me ever since I'd seen pictures in the Sunday paper of poor men selling apples for five cents each on the city streets. Those men had only a few apples to sell, but Mr. Baxter had lots of the fruit and vegetables to put on his stand and knew his neighbors would take what they wanted and leave the money in the tin bowl he kept there.

In the field beyond the stand, I saw a man pushing a wheelbarrow into a shed way down at the end.

"Look," I said to Francie. "I think it's him."

"Let's go talk to him."

Francie started down the path at the edge of the field and I followed her. "What'd you say his last name was?" she called to me. I told her, and when she got closer, she yelled out "Mr. Boudreau, Mr. Boudreau."

He lowered the wheelbarrow and turned around, looking puzzled. "Holy moly. You surprise me, you two, calling me mister," he said. "Nobody calls me mister. You, you should call me Armand like everyone else."

"And," he looked at me, "*Ça va*? You remember your French, yes?"

"Sure. *Ça va*."

"Bien, bien." Armand looked pleased. "Bien—that means good."

Then he turned to Francie. "This is your friend?"

"Yes, her name's Francie. She's my best friend."

"Hello, Francine." He said her name just like yesterday.

"No, it's Francie," I reminded him. "Her real name is Frances."

"Okay, but me, I'm gonna call her Francine. Nice French name. Yes?"

"Yes," Francie said. "Francine. Francine Cunningham. I like that."

I asked Armand if he was working for Mr. Baxter. Mr.

Baxter's vegetable fields stretched out behind his house. They got wider in back and went all the way down to the river. There were orchards there, too. Big trucks came almost every day in the summer and carried the fruit and vegetables off to the city. There used to be five or six farms on Spring Street, but when Green Glen got bigger, houses were built on most of them. Mr. Baxter's farm and Cunningham's chicken farm were the only ones left.

"Yep," Armand said. "I do some odd jobs for him and he gives me a place to sleep in the loft in the barn, he does. Sort of trying me out to see if I can work good enough to get paid."

He straightened up and pulled back his shoulder blades. When he did this, I saw a chain around his neck with a cross hanging from it. I hadn't ever seen a necklace on a man before, and it seemed kind of strange. Men wore watches and maybe a wedding band, but usually just women wore necklaces.

"Hard work," Armand continued. "But working outdoors, it's good." He took a deep breath. "The fresh air, I never worked in the fresh air before. Always indoors at the mill." He pushed the wheelbarrow all the way into the shed and stood it on end against the back wall next to a fishing pole and an old coffee can filled with dirt.

"Finished my work for today. So me, I'm goin' fishin'." He smiled at us. "You like to fish? You come, too."

Francie giggled, "Girls don't go fishing. Only boys."

Lots of times I'd wondered why girls couldn't go fishing. Most men took their sons fishing, but I didn't know of anyone who took a daughter.

"No, no, Francine. You're wrong about that." Armand pointed his finger at Francie. "Some girls are real good catching fish. My niece Marie, she's good. Bet you're just about the same age. How old are you two?"

"We're both eleven," Francie answered, "but I'm older than Charlotte because I'll be twelve in February and her birthday's not until March." The birthday part didn't seem important to me, but that was how Francie was. She couldn't help telling people everything.

"Just like I thought. Marie's eleven, too."

He picked up the fishing pole and coffee can. "I'm goin' way down around the bend there—should be a good spot." He pointed over the stone wall, across the fields of squash and pumpkins, and started walking in that direction.

"Yeah, let's go." Francie began to follow Armand. "Come on, Charlotte."

"Wait a sec. Maybe we should ask our mothers?"

"It'd take too long. We might not be able to find him when we came back." I looked at the distance back to the sidewalk and knew Francie was right.

"We won't be gone long. It'll be okay," Francie called over her shoulder as she trotted after Armand.

Yes, I guessed it would be okay. After all, Mother liked me to be outdoors after school. And today the sky was bright late-September blue. The river sparkled in the distance and seemed to say, "Come, see how beautiful I am." And I, Charlotte Bakeman, was going fishing for the first time in my life! I was glad I had met Armand Boudreau.

8

IN TROUBLE AGAIN

W e spent the rest of the afternoon along the edge of the river. It was peaceful there with the sunshine through the trees. The only sounds we heard were the murmur of the water and the afternoon chirping of those birds which had not yet gone south. I felt worlds away from Spring Street.

Armand showed us how to dangle our lines in the deep, quiet places where the trout like to hide. He had cut two poles from the willows that grew along the bank and rigged them up for us. He put the wiggly, brown worms on the hooks the first time. But when we lost them to fish which nibbled but didn't bite, he made us put the new bait on ourselves.

We talked quietly so as not to disturb the fish. Armand said that it was good of God to put fish in the river, so poor people could get something to eat without paying for it. "President Hoover, he used to talk about a chicken in every pot. But me, I like a fish in the frying pan."

"What did he mean, a chicken in every pot?" I asked.

"He meant everyone should have plenty to eat. He talked big, but lots of people stayed hungry. Still do." Armand let out a little more line. "But President Roosevelt, I think he's gonna fix it. He helps the poor people."

When I had been thinking about President Roosevelt's "nothing to fear but fear itself" speech, I didn't talk about it with my parents because I knew they didn't like Roosevelt or his ideas. In fact, I didn't know any grown-up who had ever said anything good about him. My parents felt awful when he beat Hoover in the election.

Francie looked surprised, too. "My dad says Roosevelt's ruining the country," she said. "He says the government's paying men to lean on shovels."

"Some people, they say that about the CCC. But me, I think the CCC is good," Armand said. "I'm on the waiting list, and if I'm lucky, I'll be in the CCC camp over in Manton pretty soon."

I knew the CCC was something President Roosevelt had started. Men who didn't have jobs lived in camps and went out every day to plant trees and build playgrounds and stuff like that. Dad told me CCC stood for Civilian Conservation Corps. The government paid the men for the work they did, and my father thought that was wrong.

Armand seemed to have a gift for reading my mind because he said, "Me, I think it's good they give people work. Your daddies, they both have work all the time. Big jobs. Important jobs. Maybe they don't know how bad it is to have no job. No money." I lost my bait for the third time, and he handed me the coffee can. "Everybody who wants to work should have a job. That's what I think." That made sense to me, too.

When it was time to go home, Armand had six beautiful rainbow trout strung on a willow branch, but Francie and I hadn't caught anything.

"Six trout. Two for each of us," he said. He broke off two more willow branches and put two trout on each to make it easy for us to carry them home.

"You two, you can surprise your mamas with nice fish for supper. Make them very happy," he said. We hurried home carefully holding the fish in front of us.

But Mother wasn't as happy as Armand thought she'd be, not at first anyway. There she was standing out on the sidewalk with our next-door neighbor, Mrs. Dawson, looking for me when I got back.

"Where have you been?" Mother asked. "I've been worried about you."

"We looked everywhere," Mrs. Dawson said.

"We even sent Philip and Leo out to the woods to see if you were there," Mother added. Then her voice got cross. "You can't keep doing this, Charlotte. This makes two days in a row. You *have* to let me know where you are after school."

I felt awful. I had been so happy down by the river with Armand and Francie, and now everything was turning all sour.

"For punishment," Mother continued, "you must come home right after school tomorrow and the next day and stay in your room by yourself until supper time." I knew there was no point in arguing with Mother. Once she said something like that, she didn't change her mind.

Then she noticed the fish. "Where did you get those?" she asked.

When I began to explain, she interrupted, "You mean the tramp you were talking to in the woods yesterday?"

"Well, I guess he's not a tramp anymore. He's working for Mr. Baxter now."

"Taking girls fishing," Mrs. Dawson sniffed. "Isn't that just like a Canuck? No notion of what's proper. Lazy, shiftless bunch." She almost spit the words out.

It didn't seem fair to say that about Armand, but I wasn't supposed to talk back to grown-ups. Anyway, Mother sort of did it for me. She shrugged her shoulders and said, "You could say the same things about a lot of people who aren't French."

"Well, I'm glad you're all right, Charlotte," Mrs. Dawson said. "Now I've got to get my supper started." She began to walk up her driveway.

After a few steps, she turned and said, "Take my advice, honey. Don't have anything to do with the Canucks."

Mother and I started toward the house. "Looks like we'll have fresh fish for supper," Mother said. "I love trout." At least Mother liked the fish, so maybe the afternoon wasn't so bad after all.

"Why does Mrs. Dawson talk like that about the Canucks?" I asked Mother.

"Don't use that word, Charlotte. It's better to say French Canadians." Mother sighed. "I don't know why she feels the way she does. But you have to remember that when she grew up in Green Glen, all the families were just like hers, there wasn't anybody different. Now when people speak French perhaps it seems intimidating to her because she doesn't know what they're saying." I remembered how I felt left out when Armand and Leona were speaking French. Mother began to rinse the fish. "And probably she thinks the Protestant churches which were here first are good enough for everyone, and she can't see why the mill people built a Catholic Church instead."

That seemed dumb to me. I thought people should be able to go to church wherever they wanted.

9

THE WRONG SCHOOL BUS

T he next day I stayed in my room after school. Except for not being able to talk with Francie, I didn't really mind too much. My third-floor bedroom has a window seat, where I can stretch my legs out and read, or look over at Mount Monadnock in the distance, or just daydream. I had three new library books, so I was all set. On Thursday Mother said that instead of staying home I could ride on the Mountain Road school bus and join her at her friend Mrs. Moore's, where she'd be visiting. The Moores had a big collection of *National Geographics*, and I knew I would be allowed to look at those while Mother and Mrs. Moore talked.

After school I climbed on the first of the five big yellow buses lined up along the curb, the one Miss Harris told me to take for Mountain Road. The weather had turned cold, and I was glad to get on the bus and out of the wind. I wondered if Armand could stay warm enough in Mr. Baxter's loft. Somehow I kept worrying about him. I'd never known anyone before who didn't have a house to go home to, and I couldn't imagine what that would be like.

There wasn't anyone in the driver's seat on the bus, but lots of kids were there already, shouting and throwing paper airplanes and banging their lunch boxes around.

One of the Phipps boys dangled a frog in front of a girl, just a little second-grader. He was disappointed when she wasn't scared. Instead, she scolded him for being mean to the frog. Good for her, I thought.

In a few minutes the paunchy driver heaved himself on to the bus and bellowed, "In your seats and quiet." Everyone sat down right away. I could tell he was a strict bus driver. I wanted to give him the note Mother had written, so that he'd know where to let me off, but I was afraid he'd order me to sit down before I even got up to the front.

The bus started to pull away from the curb, then the driver stopped and swung the door open. Leona Fontaine climbed on, her lunch box in one hand and her sketch pad in the other.

"Ooh, Charlotte," squealed Leona, sliding onto the seat beside me, just like I knew she would. "How come you're on my bus?"

Suddenly my stomach felt funny. Something wasn't right. If I was on Leona's bus, I was going to West Glen, not to Mountain Road. Miss Harris must have told me the wrong bus. But how could a teacher make such a terrible mistake? By the time I explained to Leona, we were half-way down Main Street, and I was on my way to being in trouble with Mother again.

"You can get off at my house with me," Leona said.

"Okay." I didn't want to go to Leona's, but at least, I could telephone Mother from there.

"Charlotte's coming to my house this afternoon," Leona twisted around and tried to sound important and impress the LaFlamme twins in the seat behind her. "Charlotte's coming to play with me today," she called across the aisle to Freddie Auclair. I wished Leona wouldn't try so hard to get everyone's attention. She didn't seem to understand why most kids didn't like her—because she was always begging for attention.

Leona lived in one of the mill workers' houses in West Glen. There were lots of them, neat and rectangular-shaped, sort of like giant versions of the houses in our new Monopoly game. They were divided in the middle, and two families each had an upstairs and a downstairs. The houses in Leona's row sat on a narrow strip of land between the river and the road.

Leona took me in through the back door. There was a stiff, shiny linoleum rug on the kitchen floor, yellow like the school bus, crisscrossed with royal blue, and the walls were a cold-looking lime green. The kitchen not only looked cold, it was cold, really cold.

Leona seemed to know what I was thinking because she said, "I'm sorry it's so cold in here. On the days when we know the pipes won't freeze, my Dad turns the stove off to save kerosene. He won't let me light it. He's afraid I'll set the house on fire." She grinned at me and shrugged her shoulders. "So I just keep my coat on until he gets home from the mill. Sometimes I wrap up in a blanket, too."

I thought of our own warm kitchen and of the cookies and milk that Mother had waiting for me when I came home from school. I wouldn't like coming home every day to a cold house and, even worse, no mother.

Leona's mother was dead, and Leona lived with her father. Rose, her older sister who was the Cunninghams' hired girl, came home once a week on her day off.

I remember the day of Leona's mother's funeral. It was

when we were in fourth grade. I pretended I needed to sharpen my pencil so I could stand by the window and see the people going into the Catholic Church across the street from the school. Leona looked very tiny. She walked beside one of her aunts with her head bent down and was dressed all in black. Even her beautiful dark curls were covered by a black veil.

Back then I thought it would be dramatic to be in Leona's place. To be dressed in black and be the center of attention, and be an orphan—well, half an orphan, anyway. Like being the heroine of a book. Like Sara Crewe in *The Little Princess*. Sara Crewe, who was poor and badly treated after her mother's death, but never lost her gentleness and imagination. Now, here in the cold kitchen, Leona's life didn't seem so dramatic.

"Let's go upstairs to my room," Leona said. "It's warmer up there because the sun comes in my window in the afternoon. I'll show you my picture books."

If Leona had talked about picture books at school, we would have made fun of her because sixth graders are much too old for picture books, but today I didn't want to hurt her feelings, so I kept quiet. Instead I said, "Okay, but first I need to phone my mother. She'll be worried about me."

Leona looked down at her feet. "We don't have a telephone," she said. I should have thought of that before. Plenty of people didn't have phones, and since the Depression lots of people had theirs taken out to save money. I should have guessed that the Fontaines wouldn't have one.

"How about one of the neighbors? Could we use theirs?"

"The Burgoynes have a phone," Leona spoke slowly,

"but I'm not allowed to leave the house until my father gets home."

"You mean you don't go outdoors to play when you get home from school?" I was thinking of how Mother was always telling me to get my nose out of a book and go out and get some fresh air.

"Yeah, my dad worries about me," Leona explained.

"But my mother's going to be worried, too. This is an emergency."

Leona took a deep breath. I could tell that she wanted to please me, but didn't want to go against her father. I thought I really should say never mind about the telephone, but I didn't because I was already in enough trouble with Mother. And I wanted to get home as soon as I could.

After a second or two, Leona said, "Yeah, I guess an emergency makes it okay." We went to the Burgoynes and phoned, and Mother said that after Dad brought her home from the Moore's, he'd drive over to West Glen and get me.

When we got back to Leona's, she started toward the stairs and said, "Now I'll show you my books."

"Is the bathroom upstairs?"

"We don't have a bathroom," Leona said. "You have to go outside to the outhouse."

I had never been at a real house without a bathroom. At my uncle's camp we used the outdoor privy, but that was a summer place.

The outhouse was even colder than the house, but I thought it was nicer than ordinary bathrooms because you could look out through the chinks in the wall and see splashes of color in two places, both in the autumn leaves across the river and their reflection in the water.

10

DRAGONS AND PRINCESSES

I went back into the house and upstairs to Leona's room. It *was* warmer there because of the sun. She pulled a large cardboard carton from under her bed, opened it, and took some neat bundles of papers out. She spread them on the bed. I realized these were the picture books she was talking about—not library books for little kids, but books someone had made by hand.

I picked one up. I could feel Leona's breath as she looked over my shoulder.

"It's a story about a dragon. The pictures show you what happens." I knew she wanted me to like it.

That wasn't hard to do. It was a wonderful book. Ten or twelve pages of white construction paper, tied together with a bright green ribbon. On the cover was a gorgeous dragon, the same bright green as the ribbon, and there were outlines of gold on the scales. Inside there were no words, just pictures. The pictures told the story of a town terrified by a frightful monster who carried off chickens and dogs and even small children. The dragon came to their rescue and killed the monster. The grateful townspeople built him a magnificent tower right in the middle of the village green. The last picture showed the dragon leaning from the uppermost turret, a satisfied look on his face and wisps of smoke curling up from his nostrils.

"Gee, Leona, this is beautiful!" I said. "Did you do this?" I knew Leona always did the best work in art class in school, and was forever scribbling on the sketch pad she carried around most of the time, but I had never seen anything like this before.

Leona beamed. "Yeah," she said, "I like to paint pictures. When Rose comes home on her day off, she helps me make them into books. Sometimes she brings me ribbon and paper and stuff, too."

"Here's one I just finished." Leona handed me another. "I call it the Book of Princesses. It isn't a story, just pictures of princesses."

I looked at it and saw princesses with yellow hair,

princesses with brown, black, and red hair. Dainty princesses. Tall, dignified princesses. Princesses dressed in shiny satin, in fur, in lace. All of them were wearing crowns and carrying scepters.

Perhaps Leona was a pest, but she surely was a good artist.

"I wish I could do something like this." I picked up another book. "I like to make up stories, too, but all I can do is words. My pictures would look terrible."

"Hey! We could do a book together," Leona's dark eyes sparkled. "You could do the words, and I'd do the pictures!" Her face had a kind of begging look.

"Yeah, maybe." I felt a little worried at the way Leona looked at me, and I was thinking of what Francie would say when she learned I was doing a book with Leona.

"We could get together every day at recess and talk about the book, and you could come home with me on the bus whenever you wanted to." Leona was excited and talking fast. "We could be best friends!" she almost shouted.

"Well, Francie's my best friend." I didn't want Leona getting the wrong idea about that. "But maybe you and I could work on a book together sometimes." I really liked the idea of doing a book with her, but I didn't want Leona the pest hanging around me all the time. For one thing, what would the other kids think—especially Francie.

Downstairs a door slammed. "Leona," a man's voice called out. "Joe Burgoyne told me you was over to his place after school." He sounded angry. "You know I don't want you out of the house—" He stopped abruptly when he saw me coming down the stairs with Leona. "Who's this?"

Leona explained how I happened to be there. Before she finished, there was a knock at the door, and there was my father.

"Charles Bakeman," he said, as he reached out his hand toward Mr. Fontaine.

Mr. Fontaine looked down at his greasy hands, "Sorry, I haven't had a chance to wash up from work yet," he said. Then neither of them seemed to know what to say next.

I went upstairs to get my coat. When I came down, the two men were talking about the Depression. That was something grown-ups could always talk about. As Dad and I started out the door, Leona grabbed my sleeve.

"Come over again tomorrow?" she asked with that pleading look in her eyes that made me feel funny.

I didn't know what to say. It would be fun to do a book with Leona. But she could be kind of creepy, and I didn't like this cold house.

Before I had time to say anything, Dad said, "Maybe Leona could come to our house tomorrow." I didn't like that idea much either, but Dad and Mr. Fontaine arranged it, and that was that.

11

STILL BEST FRIENDS

A re you crazy?" Francie said to me when I told her that Leona was coming to my house after school. "Take that Frog home with you?" "Frog" was another word for French people, like "Canuck." On the way home after school, she ran ahead with her brother instead of walking with Leona and me.

Francie and I had been best friends for years. It started when we were babies. Our mothers were good friends, and every Wednesday they did their ironing together at one house or the other, setting up their ironing boards and visiting while they worked. Over the years Francie and I grew from playpen to playroom or backyard, and finally to school. We liked to be together. I think maybe it was because we sort of balanced one another. Francie gave me courage to try new things, and I slowed her down sometimes when she got carried away with a silly idea. We always thought of ourselves as best friends. Still right now Francie was jealous, and I wished that Dad hadn't invited Leona to our house.

But I have to admit that Leona and I did have fun that afternoon. We worked until supper time on a book about a white horse. The more pictures she drew, the more ideas I got for my story.

Leona wanted to come back on Monday, but I made sure she didn't. I wasn't going to be snubbed by Francie again. And after that Francie and I walked home from school together most of the time, just as best friends should.

Over the next week or so Leona sometimes came with me, and that always made Francie mad. On those days I felt like my body was being split down the middle, with Francie pulling on one side and Leona on the other.

One day Francie and I had a big fight about it. She called Leona a Canuck mill kid and even said some of the mean things Mrs. Dawson did about the Catholics, like that they couldn't do anything unless they asked the Pope first.

I got mad and told Francie she wasn't the boss of me and couldn't tell me what to do. Then I ran ahead and wouldn't walk home with her that day. I was tired of Francie not even trying to understand Leona. It seemed as if she thought they couldn't be friends just because Leona was French Canadian and lived in West Glen. I knew Francie was walking up the Spring Street hill a few feet behind me, but I just kept on going.

When I got to Baxter's, Armand's voice came booming down from the ladder where he was replacing a bulb in the outdoor light. "What is this, you two? Some new kind of parade you're doing?"

"I'm just walking home from school," I said, trying to pretend there was nothing out of the ordinary.

Armand stepped down from the ladder.

"But you don't walk together, you and Francine. How come? You two, you always walk together like the animals in Noah's Ark."

"Sometimes Francie thinks she's the boss of the whole world." I turned my head a little and said it loud enough for Francie to hear. Even though I didn't turn all the way around, I knew she was standing not far behind me at the end of the driveway.

Armand lifted his cap and scratched his head. "Seems like something's wrong with you, Charlotte. And you, Francine, I never seen you when you don't have something to say."

"All she wants to do is write stories so that pesty Canuck kid can draw the pictures." Francie glared at me. "She doesn't want to be my best friend anymore."

"Not true, Francie! I do still want to be best friends with you. I just don't want you to boss me."

But Armand didn't seem to care about the best friend part. He scowled at Francie. "What's all this Canuck talk?" he asked. "Me, I don't like that word."

"You know what I mean. The kids from West Glen— they're sort of well—crude."

"You think I'm crude, Francine?" Armand looked right at Francie. "Me," Armand continued, "I'm a Canuck, too."

"But I didn't mean you."

"I didn't think you did. But when you say Canuck, it hurts all of us." Armand looked at Francie as if he wanted to be sure she understood. Then his face relaxed.

"Okay. Enough of that. Let's hear the rest of this problem," he said.

We told him the whole story about Leona and the books. Sometimes we took turns, and sometimes we both talked at once.

Armand listened, nodding his head and saying those "mon der" words from time to time.

When we got to the part about the fight, Armand said, "Enough, enough. I keep hearing best-friend talk here. Charlotte, she wants to be Francine's best friend, and Francine, she wants to be Charlotte's." He pulled the ladder down and got ready to carry it back to the shed.

"So, *ça va*. Go on home and have some cookies and milk together the way best friends are supposed to."

Francie and I didn't say anything to each other, but we started walking down the sidewalk together.

"*Ça va*," Armand called after us.

12

THE MISSING RADIO

After the cookies and milk, we went to Francie's and walked out to the chicken house to ride on the feed trolley. That's one of our favorite things to do after school.

A feed trolley is a thick board about six feet long and a foot and a half wide. It's attached by heavy ropes to tracks which run along the ceiling the whole length of the chicken house. Alan and Butch put buckets of grain and water on the trolley and push or pull it from room to room, stopping in each section to fill the troughs where the chickens eat and drink. When Francie and I were little, we used to just sit on the trolley and ride. But now we stand on it and hop off to help fill the feeders.

"I seen you girls talking to that tramp the other day," Alan said in an accusing voice as soon as we walked in.

"He's not a tramp anymore," Francie told him. "He's working for Mr. Baxter now."

"Not regular," Alan snapped back. "Only helping with the fall chores. And you kids better watch out. Probably he's a thief, too."

"Whad'ya mean?" Francie asked.

"Well, I don't want to talk about a guy behind his back." I could tell Alan really did want to talk. He was tall, with blue eyes, and hair that looked like straw. He was the leader in anything he and Butch did, especially if it was teasing or making trouble. Butch was quieter and had a soft, round face. We liked him better than Alan. But usually he went along with whatever Alan said.

"Things have been missing." Alan paused and seemed to be waiting to be asked for details. A cloud of light brown grain dust spread into the air as he emptied a sack into one of the buckets.

"What things? What're you talking about?" Francie sounded annoyed.

"I'm talking about the radio Butch and I listen to in the egg room. You know, when we're working down there."

"Yeah."

"It got all staticky the other day. Something wrong with it. Your dad said he'd get Jim Barnes to fix it." Alan pushed the trolley into the first section. The chickens were clucking and getting underfoot so that you had to wade through them to fill their troughs.

"We set the radio on the side porch for Jim to pick up— but when Jim got there—no radio." He gave the last two words extra emphasis. "Not a sign of it." He paused and looked at us as if we should be impressed.

"So, what happened to it?" asked Francie.

I wished Alan would get to the point. At the same time I thought I knew what he was going to say and I didn't like it.

"I dunno. No one knows. Except maybe your tramp friend. It was the same day he brought back the lawn mower that the Baxters borrowed. Had to push it right by the side porch on his way to the shed."

"Keep the grain in the trough," Butch scolded, as Francie emptied a bucket a little too fast.

"He musta seen that radio setting there and thought it was a good chance to get himself one," Alan continued.

That made me mad, but before I could get my courage up to say anything, Francie chimed in.

"He wouldn't do that. I know he wouldn't."

We hopped back on the trolley as it moved into the next section.

"That's right. He wouldn't do that," I echoed.

"Don't you girls be fooled by him," Butch said. "Just because he has those big brown eyes and talks polite to you."

"The real thing is where else could the radio have gone?" Alan looked at us as if he thought he had proved his point.

"I dunno," Francie hesitated. "Lots of things could have happened to it."

"Yeah, well—you find out what, you let me know." We worked in silence for a few minutes, filling the troughs in the second section.

"These Canucks really get me," Alan said as we were going into the third section. "Think the world owes 'em a living. Think they can just help themselves to other people's stuff. Probably they'll be thinking they can take our jobs away next."

I was glad there was only one section left in the first chicken house. I'd leave after that. I thought Francie must have had enough of Alan by now, too.

"Me and Butch are thinking of going over to Baxter's barn and getting that radio back." Alan nudged the hens away from the trough with his boot.

"Stupid biddies, get out of the way. How do you think I can get the feed in if you're right under my feet?" he sputtered. "That's where the Canuck's sleeping, you know. Mr. Baxter's letting him use the loft."

As soon as we got out of the chicken house, I told Francie we had to warn Armand. She agreed. We looked all over as much of Baxter's farm as we could before it was time to go home for supper, but we didn't find him.

13

A BAD WEEK ON SPRING STREET

W e didn't see Armand until the next afternoon. He was unloading a wheelbarrow of orange Hubbard squashes onto the vegetable stand and most of his head was covered with a big white bandage.

"What happened to your head?" we both asked at once.

"Had some trouble last night."

"Was it Alan and Butch?"

"Yeah, how'd you know?"

We told him about what had been said in the chicken house. We talked fast and kept interrupting each other, telling Armand how sorry we were that we hadn't found him in time to warn him.

"Thank goodness Mr. Baxter, he heard the noise and he stopped 'em. Going at me in the dark—like animals, them two." Armand shook his head as if he couldn't believe what had happened. "Holy moly. Lucky they didn't hurt me no worse than they did."

I couldn't believe it either, couldn't believe Butch and Alan would be so mean.

"Dr. Peavey, he put six stitches in the back of my head. Had to shave off a lot of hair to do it." He started to push the wheelbarrow. Then he set it down with an angry thump. "What gets me is they still think I took their radio. Think I hid it or sold it. I never seen that radio! I told 'em so. Mr. Baxter, he believes me." Armand lifted the handles of the wheelbarrow again. "I'll get even with them guys sometime," he muttered. "I tell you, I will."

It was a bad week on upper Spring Street. Everyone was talking about the stolen radio. Mr. Cunningham thought the circumstances made Armand a suspect, but of course he didn't approve of Butch and Alan attacking him they way they had. Mrs. Dawson said several times that you can't trust the Canucks, and she had always said so. Mrs. Brewster wondered what the world was coming to, if you couldn't leave something on your porch and expect to find it there when you came back. Rose thought everyone suspected Armand just because he was French. Butch, who was sweet on Rose, got jealous when she stood up for Armand.

Then just when it seemed that things couldn't get any worse something happened to Leona's father. Mr. Fontaine's arm was crushed in one of the machines at the mill, and he had to be in the hospital for two weeks. Since there was no one else at home, Leona came to stay with Rose at the Cunninghams' until her father was better. So whether Francie liked it or not, she had Leona right there in her house, staying in Rose's room.

And that meant that Leona was tagging along with Francie and me after school. We didn't feel like being around Alan and Butch after the way they'd attacked Armand, so we stayed away from the chicken houses. Instead we went out in the woods to the Hideaway.

Before, when Francie and I were there, we'd get our books out of the metal box and spend most of our time reading. When Leona was with us, it was different. She wanted to do baby things, like play "make-believe". One day she stood at the edge of the brook and said we should pretend she was Eliza crossing the ice. We all knew Eliza because Miss Harris was reading us a chapter from *Uncle Tom's Cabin* every day after lunch, but Francie and I felt too old to play a pretend game about it.

"That's a dumb idea," Francie told her. "In some places we can jump across easy as pie."

"It's too warm for ice," I added.

"But it's fun to make-believe." Leona looked hurt. Then she spotted some old pieces of plywood under an alder bush. She grabbed one and dragged it over to the brook. "See, here's the ice!" She hopped on and shouted back to us as she teetered on the slab of plywood, "You can be Simon Legree and come chasing after me."

Floating on the plywood did look like fun, and since

there wasn't anybody else out there in the woods to see us, we joined in. Francie launched herself into the brook and went pushing after Leona. And, of course, I followed her. That meant there were two Simon Legrees chasing one Eliza, so we took turns being Eliza, and it worked fine. I had a good time that afternoon, and I was glad that Francie seemed to have fun with Leona, too. Maybe both of us were beginning to think of her as a friend instead of a pest.

On Thursday when the three of us were playing jacks on the Cunninghams' side porch, the dry cleaner delivery man came. Mrs. Cunningham opened the door and gave him the clothes that needed cleaning.

He started down the path, then turned and called to her, "Did you find where I put the radio last week?"

"What?" said Mrs. Cunningham, coming out onto the porch.

"Where?" All three of us jumped up.

Everyone started moving toward the dry cleaner man. He looked surprised.

"I'm sorry," he said. "I meant to call, but it slipped my mind." We were waiting for what he was going to say next. "No one was here, so I just hung the clothes inside the door. It looked like rain, and I saw that nice little radio sitting there on the edge of the porch and thought to myself, it'd be a shame for that to get wet, so I put it inside that box there." He pointed to the big wooden chest where the Cunninghams kept badminton racquets, baseball gloves, and other sports stuff.

Francie and Leona and I practically flew across the porch.

"Here it is!" exclaimed Francie.

"See, Armand didn't take it!" I was jumping all over the place.

"I've got to go tell Rose." Leona went running off.

"We told you so!" Francie was cradling the radio and jumping around, too. "Armand didn't take it."

"All right, girls, quiet down," Mrs. Cunningham said. "Thank you, Mr. Bertrand. That was really thoughtful of you to put the radio under cover. And now you've helped us solve a mystery, too, because we wondered what had happened to it. Thanks again."

He looked puzzled, shrugged his shoulders, and walked back to his van.

14

LEONA AND MISS COLLINS

One afternoon before Columbus Day Francie and I were climbing in the Cunninghams' beech tree. When I got close to the top, I could look down and see Francie up almost as high as I was, and Leona way down below sitting on the grass working on one of the sketches she was forever doing. The blue sky and crisp air made me feel like singing or shouting.

"Behind him lay the gray Azores!" I called out. It was the first line of a poem about Columbus which Miss Harris was having us memorize.

"Behind him the Gates of Hercules!" Francie answered loud and clear with the next line.

"Brave Admiral, speak: what shall I say?" That was my line.

"Why, say: Sail on! Sail on! And on!" came Francie's reply, loud and lively. It was the kind of brisk fall weather that made you feel like shouting.

We giggled at how

good we were, and did it all over again. "Sail on! Sail on! And on!"

Then we heard Miss Collins over the stone wall which separated her yard from the Cunninghams'.

"Hey, you there." Francie and I climbed down from the tree to see what she wanted. But it was Leona she was calling.

"Yes, you," she pointed at Leona. That was Miss Collins' way of talking, sort of gruff and quick.

She was an artist, an old woman who lived by herself in the house next to the Cunninghams'. She'd grown up in that house long ago when it was part of her father's farm, but she had gone off to Boston to study art when she was a young woman. When her parents were ill toward the end of their lives, she came back to take care of them and then stayed on by herself after they died. It was a good quiet place to work, she told Mother, and as long as she could get to the Museum of Fine Arts in Boston three or four times a year (which she did), Green Glen was a fine place for her to be.

Miss Collins didn't like children much. We all knew that, and we all knew not to go into her yard or even to play in the field next to her house.

Twice a year, once during Christmas vacation and once in the summer, Miss Collins invited Mother and me for tea. It was always the same, and I loved it. Miss Collins would usher us down a long hall, past the parlor filled with old-fashioned furniture, past the studio where she painted, taking us into the library because that's where the doll house was, the one she had when she was a little girl. First we were served tea, real tea for Mother and Miss Collins and warm milk with a touch of tea for me.

When I was little, and while Mother and Miss Collins talked, I was allowed to play with the beautiful, old-fashioned dollhouse. I moved the little pieces of furniture around, took small coats and aprons out of a miniature trunk and changed the dolls' clothes, arranged tiny bits of plaster food on their plates, even lifted the lids of the black kitchen stove with a tool made just for that purpose.

"Hey, girl, what are you doing?" Miss Collins called again.

"Nothing, Miss Collins." Leona looked scared. She knew how Miss Collins felt about children. "I'm just making a drawing."

"Come here. Let me see."

Leona walked over to the stone wall and handed her pad across to Miss Collins.

"Um," Miss Collins nodded, then flipped through the other pages, stopping now and then for a closer look. "I guess you like to draw?" she said to Leona.

"Oh, yes, better than anything in the world!"

"Well, I think you should come and have a look around my studio. Maybe try some paints. Would you like that?"

"Oh, yes, I would!"

I couldn't believe that Miss Collins was actually inviting Leona to come into her house, into her studio, even. I'd never been in the studio, just looked in the door as we walked by. That made me jealous.

"Can Charlotte and I come, too?" Francie asked. I wouldn't have dared to ask, but Francie did.

"No," Miss Collins barked. "One girl at a time is enough. Besides, you two don't have portfolios like this girl." I don't think she even knew Leona's name, and I guess what she meant by portfolio was Leona's sketch pad.

So Leona walked around the stone wall and followed Miss Collins into her house. Francie and I didn't feel like climbing any more. The truth is we felt left out.

15

THE SPRING STREET HERALD

When I woke up on Saturday the next week, I heard the rain pounding on the roof over my third-floor bedroom. It had rained yesterday and the day before, and it was still raining! This was the day we were supposed to climb Mount Monadnock with the Cunninghams. We did it every October, the Bakemans and the Cunninghams. But today the rain would spoil everything. It would be a boring, rainy, indoor Saturday.

I was still dawdling over my oatmeal and feeling glum about the day when Francie and Leona came over. They plopped themselves down at the kitchen table, and the water dripping off their raincoats made puddles on the floor.

A few minutes later my dad appeared at the kitchen door. "Emma," he called, "since we can't climb the mountain today, I'm going down to the office for a while." Then, noticing Francie and Leona and me, he said, "You girls look as if the world had come to an end." He buttoned up his raincoat. "Too bad you don't have a newspaper office to go to."

"Maybe they do." Mother's voice came from the pantry. I wondered what she meant. "It's a good day for a home newspaper," Mother said as she brought a bag of flour from the pantry and set it down on the kitchen table.

I was still feeling grumpy because we couldn't climb the mountain, but Francie said, "Hey, yeah! Let's do a newspaper. We can use the barn as our office."

Once our place had been a farm. There wasn't hay in the barn anymore, and there weren't any animals, but there were lots of nifty places to play.

"The horse stalls would be good," Francie continued. "You and I can get the stories. Maybe get scoops like Nancy Drew did in the book I just finished."

Leona said she could do pictures and Francie said that would be good. We both felt a little different about Leona since Miss Collins had been giving her painting lessons. She went to Miss Collins' studio almost every day after school now. She liked going there, and you could tell it made her feel important. She knew Francie and I were envious of her.

Dad said that when he came home for lunch, he'd bring a few sheets of newsprint so we could paste up our stories to look like a real newspaper.

The idea began to grow. I remembered a paper that my cousins had made last winter when there was no school because of a blizzard.

It didn't take us long to turn the horse stall into an office. We put a board across two orange crates to make a desk. And we used a couple more orange crates for chairs. We found paper and pencils. Leona began to work on a sign which would be tacked on the wall and say *The Spring Street Herald*.

"Let's begin with a *Locals* column," Francie said, picking up a pencil. *The Green Glen Weekly* always had several columns of *Locals* in between the other news. "Mrs. Arthur Jones of Kent was a guest at the home of Mr. and Mrs. James Cunningham this past weekend." Francie spoke the words out loud as she wrote them. "That's my grandmother," she explained.

"I know," I said, "don't you think I know your grandmother's name?" When people have been best friends since they were babies, they know all about one another.

I looked at what Francie had written.

"Hold up a minute. We can't do handwriting, we've got to print, and we've got to make it just as wide as a newspaper column. Then we can cut it and paste it on to the newsprint, and it'll all come out even. That's how my cousins did it."

We measured a column in *The Green Glen Weekly* and then drew columns two-and-a-half inches wide on the paper we were going to use, and began printing out *Locals*. We wrote about Mr. Fontaine's accident, the Brewsters' cat having kittens, Miss Collins getting her stone wall repaired, the Monadnock hike being postponed, and other items of interest to the Cunninghams and Bakemans and Fontaines.

"We need some longer articles," I said, "some real news stories."

Francie agreed. "We've got to go out and be reporters. Reporters go out rain or shine."

"I'm staying right here," Leona said. "I can't draw in the rain."

Francie and I got into our raincoats, and I found a couple pads of paper and gave Francie one. "You do your side of the street, and I'll do mine." I put the pad in my raincoat pocket to keep it dry.

"Okay. Meet you back here in half an hour," Francie said.

I didn't go all the way down Spring Street, just as far as Brewsters', and worked my way back up from there. The only news Mrs. Brewster could think of was that her daughter and son-in-law from Boston would be visiting next weekend. I wrote it down, but it would be another local. I was looking for a longer story, something more exciting.

I sloshed through the puddles and Mrs. Baxter gave me an idea for a longer story, the Jamboree, which would be held next week. It was a carnival to benefit the hospital, the big fall event in Green Glen. I could write a lot about that.

"You can mention that I'm going to be selling my crochet work in the Arts and Crafts section, if you want," Mrs. Baxter added.

But the big scoop came from Mrs. Dawson. I asked if she had any news, and did she ever! Big news. Well, maybe not as exciting as when Nancy Drew found out about the bank robbers, but certainly the most exciting thing that had happened on Spring Street for a while.

Mrs. Dawson had been cleaning out Mr. Dawson's closet. Although he had died over a year ago, up until now she hadn't sorted out his clothes because, she said, touching them made her cry. But the church had asked for donations of clothes for people who were having a hard time because of the Depression. "And," she said, "it seemed sinful for Walter's clothes just to be hanging here, not doing anyone any good. He wouldn't have wanted it that way."

Among the stuff in the closet she had found some old coveralls. "Must have been the ones he wore the last day he worked," she said. They were too greasy to clean up enough for anyone else to wear. She had lifted up the lid on the stove and was about to pitch them into the wood fire when she decided to check the pockets for handkerchiefs. She didn't find any handkerchiefs, but she did find a ten dollar bill. And to think she had almost heaved it into the fire!

She showed it to me and said, "I'm going to use it to pay George Hill to come over to fix the leak in the roof, like I've been wanting to. It's almost as if Walter's still taking care of me." Mrs. Dawson wiped away a tear.

"Windfall for Mrs. Dawson." I was composing the headline and lead sentence in my mind as I walked back to the barn.

16

TROUBLE IN THE EGG ROOM

B ack at the barn Francie had only one story to report. She had walked up to the dirt road beyond our house and discovered that the brook was running over the road on the way to Watsons'. "If the culvert had caved in and Mr. Watson's car had fallen in the hole, it would be a better story," Francie complained. To make up for the lack of big news she suggested a gossip column. "Like Louella Parsons in the Boston paper, you know?"

"But we don't know any gossip."

"Well, we can say something like, 'A little bird told me that the sons of two prominent Spring Street families were the ones who forgot to close the gate to Mr. Card's pasture the day the cows got out and trampled Mr. Baxter's corn.'"

"You mean Philip and Leo? Everybody already knows that."

"That was just an example. Leave the gossip column to me. I'll come up with something."

Francie worked on the gossip column and in my neatest printing I carefully copied the stories I had collected. Leona was drawing a picture of Mrs. Dawson holding up the ten-dollar bill. The only sound in the horse-stall office was the rain beating against the side of the barn.

By the time Dad came home at noon with the newsprint we were ready to cut and paste and put the paper together. After the first one was done, we made a second, so that both households could have a copy. It was too much work to make any more. Leona could use the Cunninghams', and other people who wanted to read the paper would have to borrow one.

I couldn't help feeling proud when I looked at *The Spring Street Herald*, full of news, resting on the dining-room table. It hadn't been a bad day after all, and now the rain was letting up, too.

"Charlotte," Mother called from the kitchen where she was fixing supper, "I don't have enough eggs for the muffins. Run over to Cunninghams' and get me a dozen, please." Cunninghams' was mainly a hatchery for baby chicks, but Francie's father sold a few eggs in the basement of the incubator building. He did it as a convenience for the neighbors, the same way Mr. Baxter did with his vegetable stand.

When I started down the stairs to the egg room, I heard music from the radio. The same radio which had caused so much trouble. It was fixed now and back on the shelf.

And I heard voices, too. One was Butch's. Francie and I had been avoiding Butch and Alan since they had beaten up Armand, but if I had to talk to one of them, I preferred Butch. His round face sometimes reminded me of the cherub on the plate which hung in my grandmother's dining room. But he certainly hadn't acted like a cherub the other night.

The second voice belonged to Rose. I wasn't surprised that Rose was in the egg room because everyone knew that she liked Butch. Whenever she had a chance, she would hang around where he was. Francie and I giggled about it sometimes.

I stopped on the stairs because Butch was shouting and it sounded like Rose was crying. "I'm not good enough for you, huh?" Butch yelled. He folded his arms and glared at Rose. "You Canucks all stick together. Right?"

"I don't know..." Rose could barely choke the words out between the sobs. "I don't know," she started again, "what you're talking about." The last two words were all mixed up with her crying.

"You promised to go to the Jamboree with me." Butch picked a paper up from the counter and waved it in front of Rose. "Then this Canuck Romeo comes along, and you take up with him."

I felt funny because it didn't seem right to be eavesdropping on Rose and Butch. I started to tiptoe up the stairs, but turned and looked again. Of course, the paper which Butch was waving in front of Rose was the Cunninghams' copy of *The Spring Street Herald*. I stopped, frozen, two steps from the top.

"Listen to this." Butch held the paper in front of him and read, "Last week an honest man was beaten up by two local farm workers whose initials are A and B. The victim has vowed revenge. Rumor has it that he has already captured the heart of B's girlfriend."

Rose stopped crying to listen. "What is that thing?" She snatched at the paper.

Butch held on to it and pushed her hand away. "Wait," he said, "there's more. Perhaps you'll see the happy couple together at the Jamboree next week."

I didn't wait to hear any more. I raced upstairs, out of the incubator building and toward the Cunninghams' house. I found Francie on the back porch.

"Francie, you've got to come straighten things out between Butch and Rose." Grabbing her by the hand, I yanked her toward the egg room.

When we got there, Butch had turned his back on Rose and was shifting eggs from a wire basket into egg cartons. Just as we came down the stairs, he slammed one down too hard and made a mess of broken egg on the counter.

Rose was bent over *The Spring Street Herald*, softly sounding out the words in the gossip column, using her finger to guide her. She looked up when we came down the stairs. Her eyes were red from crying. But even with red eyes Rose was pretty. I would love to change my straight mouse-brown hair for Rose's thick black curls. She and Leona both had beautiful hair.

"Did you girls do this thing?" Rose shook the paper at us. "What does this mean?"

Butch whirled around. He was angry, no doubt about it. "It means," he said, "that you've been making eyes at that Canuck over at Baxters'."

"Gosh, Butch," Francie sounded annoyed. "Don't be

silly. It's only a joke. I was just trying to make the gossip column a little more interesting."

"Some joke," Rose said, grabbing Francie by the shoulders and pulling her so that they faced each other. "You gotta learn, Francie, that other folks have feelings, too."

I couldn't believe that this was the same Rose who was usually so gentle. No wonder Francie looked scared.

"I'm sorry, Rose." Francie didn't sound annoyed any more. She sounded afraid. In fact, I thought she might cry. But she didn't. Instead she took a deep breath and said, "I didn't mean to make trouble. I was just trying to add some excitement to our newspaper."

"Well, you *did* make a lot of trouble." Butch was almost snarling. "And now you've got me thinking about it, maybe this Armand guy *is* gonna try to take Rose away from me. Maybe that's how he'll get back at me."

"Oh, Butch. He's a nice fellow, but I don't like him the way I like you." Rose lifted her dark brown eyes toward Butch. Just then Mrs. Cunningham called from the back porch. "I gotta get going," Rose said and started up the stairs. "Just forget about it," she called over her shoulder.

"When the deep purple falls over sleepy garden walls," crooned the radio in the background

"I ain't gonna forget about it," Butch muttered. "That guy tries anything with Rose—I'll give him some more of what he got before."

17

THE ACCIDENT

Since the trouble about the radio and the newspaper Francie and I hadn't been riding the feed trolleys after school. We didn't really like being around Alan and Butch anymore. Mr. Fontaine was home from the hospital, and most days Leona was either at home with him or at Miss Collins' studio.

So it was just Francie and me together again most of the time. On warm days we went to the Hideaway. And, when there was a cold snap the week before Thanksgiving, we went skating in the field out behind the chicken houses. It was a low place that flooded over and froze and was safe for skating early in the winter, but we had to dodge the stubble which stuck up through the ice in places. We would have preferred Brewster's Pond. It was bigger and the ice was smoother, but we promised our parents not to go there because it wasn't frozen deep enough yet.

One afternoon when we were sitting on a log in the field by the edge of the ice lacing up our skates, we heard a man yelling. He was coming from way over on the other side, running and waving his hands wildly and shouting, but we couldn't tell what he was saying.

"Who's that?" I stood up to get a better view, my ankles wobbling because I hadn't finished lacing my skates.

"Gee whilikers, it looks like Butch." Francie stood up, too.

"Hey...kids...help." It *was* Butch and he was out of breath, but now he was getting close enough so we could hear what he was saying.

"What's wrong?" Francie leaned forward and screamed.

Butch stopped on the other side of the ice, gasping for air. "Alan's in Brewster's Pond, and I can't get him out." Butch took a deep breath. "He's too far away." Butch's voice quavered. "I gotta get back. Find someone to help." He looked at Francie, who had sat back down on the log and was tugging at her skates. "I think your father's at the breeders' meeting—so tell your mother. Find someone. But do it quick! I gotta get back to Alan." Butch's voice was frantic. "Mr. Baxter, maybe. Hurry!" He started to run back, then turned and shouted even louder, "Hurry!"

We got our shoes on as fast as we could. Butch knew perfectly well that Mr. Cunningham was away for the afternoon, and that was why he and Alan had sneaked off from work to go ice fishing. But that wasn't important now. The important thing was to find someone who could get Alan out of the pond. His life might actually depend on Francie and me!

We ran faster than we ever had in the races in gym class. And the thoughts in my head were going fast, too—wondering how long Alan could hold out in the cold water, trying to think of who we'd find to help, realizing that this was the first time in my life I had ever been so important.

When we got to Cunninghams' house, Francie sort of choked. "I'll tell Mother." She was so out of breath she could barely speak. "You..." She pointed down the street in the direction of Baxter's. I nodded and kept running.

Armand was sorting and trimming cabbages in Baxter's barn. He looked up, smiled and asked, "*Ça va,* Charlotte?"

But this was no time for French. I told him, in little spurts of words, what had happened, while I tried to get rid of the tight feeling in my chest so I could breathe again. Armand said Mr. Baxter wasn't home and continued to put the cabbages into their crates.

"You've *got* to come!" I yelled.

"Them fellows don't want my help."

"But Armand," I grabbed his arm and tugged at it, "Alan may be drowning. You've *got* to come!" I shrieked.

He stood up quickly, sending cabbages rolling across the barn floor. Thank goodness he was going to help. He was outside in no time and running far ahead of me.

There was no way I could keep up with him.

18

THE RESCUE

When I got to Brewster's Pond, I saw Armand crouched at the edge, shoving a big plank over the frozen part of the pond. Only Alan's head and shoulders were above water. His elbows were on the ice, holding him up, but pieces of ice were breaking off and falling into the water beside him, so he had to keep moving his arms in order to stay afloat. His face was the same color as the gray sky beyond him and his head was beginning to roll to one side.

"We're going to get you. Don't worry. We're going to get you." I heard Armand calling, almost crooning, to Alan.

"Grab the plank," Francie shouted. She and Butch were crouched down beside Armand.

But instead of grabbing the plank, Alan closed his eyes and his head lolled even farther to the side.

Armand's voice changed abruptly. "Hey, stay awake. Stay awake," he shouted. "We can't help you unless you stay awake." He moved the plank right next to Alan's hands. "Grab it. Grab it NOW," he ordered.

Alan opened his eyes and took hold of the plank. Thank goodness. I sighed a huge sigh and heard Francie and Butch do the same.

Alan hitched the upper part of his body onto the plank. Armand and Butch began to pull it in. They worked slowly because Alan's head had flopped down on the plank and he was barely holding on anymore. I was afraid he might roll off. But at last Armand and Butch got him close enough so they could grab him and pull him in.

I was so intent on watching the rescue I hadn't noticed that Mrs. Cunningham was there with an armful of blankets. She spread one on the ground and Armand and Butch lifted Alan onto it and wrapped him up. She had brought the farm truck down the track to the edge of the field and carried the blankets from there.

Alan seemed groggy. Mrs. Cunningham said they must get him to Dr. Peavey's right away. She hurried back across the field to turn the motor on and get the cab warmed up. Armand and Butch clasped arms together to make a seat and carried Alan to the truck, the same way I'd seen the high school boys carry their star player off the field after a football game. Francie and I brought the extra blankets. Francie kept asking Alan how he felt, but the one time his eyes were open, he just waved away her question.

Armand and Butch tucked Alan into the cab beside Mrs. Cunningham and put the extra blankets around him. Then they jumped into the back and pulled us up there, too.

"Wow, that was close." Butch put his hands to his face and shook his head. It seemed like he was trying to get his thoughts straight. Then he brought his hands down to hold on to the side of the truck as we bounced up the farm road toward the street. We all had to hold on tight to keep from bouncing out.

Butch looked at Armand. "Lucky thing you were around today. And lucky thing you thought to pick up that plank."

"I remembered when I was a little kid. My father, he got my Uncle Maurice out of the river that way. Just came sort of natural to pick up that plank." Then he looked at Francie and me. "Even better thing these girls were around and good thing they run so fast."

Butch said we were really good kids. Then he turned toward Armand. "Never thought I'd be glad to see you." He paused and looked right at Armand's eyes. "That's just being honest," he explained. "But I sure was today. That's being honest, too." I had never heard Butch sound so serious. By then we were off the bumpy farm road and on our way down Spring Street which was smoother. Then Butch and Armand could let go of the truck sides long enough to shake hands, which was sort of strange to see.

Armand grinned. "I'm glad I was here, I am." He looked at Butch. "Funny thing," he said. "I've been trying to think of how to get even with you two guys. But now I don't think I need to get even any more." The truck was at the bottom of Spring Street and turning on to School Street for Dr. Peavey's office. "Maybe today will make things better between us?" He looked at Butch for an answer.

"Seems so." Butch spoke slowly.

When they helped Alan out of the truck, he was still pale and shaky, but he looked better than he had at the pond.

"Where's the Canuck?" he asked. "I want to thank the Canuck..." he paused, "for saving my life."

I wished he hadn't said "Canuck," and I gritted my teeth and, almost under my breath, I said, "His name is Armand."

Alan must have heard me because he said, "That's right, I want to thank Armand."

19

STILL A SCAREDY CAT

Charlotte, hey Charlotte." Leona jumped off the bus and ran across the playground toward me. The wind, warm for late November, was blowing her dark brown hair around her face, and she was waving her sketch book.

"Clowns," Leona squealed as she came closer. "I made lots of clown pictures so you could do a story about them." She opened her sketch book to show me.

I was torn between wanting to look at Leona's drawings and wanting to get into a game of hopscotch. On the girls' side of Green Glen School hopscotch was definitely the big thing, before school, at recess, or any time we had a few minutes outside. And the unseasonably warm weather after Thanksgiving this year gave us a chance for a few more days of hopscotch before snow came and covered the playground.

I wanted to rush over and get a place in one of the games, but Leona was my friend now, and I didn't want to hurt her feelings. And I really did want to see what she had drawn. When I looked, I saw lots of clowns. I especially liked the little boy clown. He had red hair and a freckled face, full of mischief. The kind of face that made you think he'd enjoy playing tricks on the other clowns, and probably the rest of the circus people, too. A story was already beginning in my mind, but I also had an eye on the hopscotch game.

"I'll do the story tonight and bring it back tomorrow," I told Leona.

"Maybe I could stop at your house the next time I go to Miss Collins and give you some more ideas," she said.

Leona liked to come to my house, and she liked having milk and cookies at the kitchen table. She told me that if her mother was still alive, there would always be milk and cookies at her house, too.

Leona and I headed toward the hopscotch game, but the bell rang before we got there.

When it was time for recess, the teachers lined us up inside and we walked quietly down the big wide staircase to the door which led out into the playground. The boys turned and walked through the hall to their door on the other side of the building. But once out our door we girls raced pell mell to find hopscotch places, and I was determined to get into a game this time.

I found a good spot with Francie and a couple other girls. I was first, and when I was hopping through the squares, Leona came and asked to join our group, instead of sketching as she usually did. I said, "Sure," but the other girls said we already had four and that was enough, so she wandered off along the paved part of the playground looking for another place. I was just giving up my turn to Francie when I heard Alice's whiney voice.

"Don't even bother to ask us. We don't play with mackerel snappers." I went all sweaty. People who didn't like Catholics sometimes called them "mackerel snappers" because it was a rule of their church for them to eat fish instead of meat on Fridays. How could Alice be so mean?

"Yeah," Miriam said. "We don't want anybody who has to ask the Pope if it's all right for her to play hopscotch." All the kids around heard Miriam and Alice. Some of them giggled, even some of the Catholic kids.

"I didn't want to play with you anyway," Leona sort of spit the words out at Alice. She turned and ran fast toward a shady corner of the playground where a bunch of fourth graders were making snowballs out of a patch of snow which hadn't been washed away by yesterday's rain.

When the sixth grade filed in after recess, I saw that Leona's eyes were red, and I knew that Alice and Miriam had made her cry. Darn them!

Spelling lesson began, but I couldn't concentrate. I kept thinking about what had happened on the playground. I had a chance to stick up for my friend, and I hadn't done it. I wished I had walked straight over to Miriam and Alice and let them know they couldn't get away with talking to Leona like that. But of course I was too much of a scaredy cat to do it. Why couldn't I be brave? Why couldn't I stick up for my friend when she needed help? I felt miserable.

The sound of giggling brought me out of my daydreaming and back into the classroom. Miss Harris must have called on me because everyone was looking at me.

"Charlotte, can you tell us what *malice* means?" Miss Harris asked. "That's what I asked you before," she added gently.

I found *malice* on my spelling list. "Desire to see another suffer," I read from my notebook. Miss Harris always had us look up the dictionary meaning and write it down. Easy to spell. Easy to remember, too. Just like Alice, only with an M at the beginning. In fact, I thought, that's what her name should be, not Alice, but Malice.

20

NOTHING TO FEAR BUT FEAR ITSELF

W hen I came out of the building after school that afternoon, there was a commotion around the West Glen bus. Miriam and Alice were in the middle of it. They walked to school and shouldn't even be near the buses. But there they were, picking on Leona again.

"Mackerel snapper." Now I was close enough to hear. "Go on home to where the mackerel snappers live." Leona was in tears. She pushed Eddie Burgoyne out of the way and scrambled onto the bus so fast that she fell against the top step and sent her sketch pad sailing into the aisle and her lunch box under the front seat. Miriam and Alice giggled.

This was too much for me. I felt bad that I had not stood up to them before. I didn't want to be a coward again. I squeezed by the other kids and planted myself in front of Miriam and Alice.

"You're mean!" I put my hands on my hips and shoved my face in front of theirs.

"You think you're better than she is! Just because she lives in a different place and goes to a different church than you do!" I couldn't believe I was actually screaming at the Terrible Twosome. I guess Miriam and Alice couldn't believe it either because for a moment they just stared at me. And I caught a quick glimpse of a wide-eyed Leona watching through the bus window.

Then Alice snarled, "Get out of the way."

"No, I won't!" I felt like pushing her right down on the ground, but I didn't want to fight her, I wanted to make her listen. I wanted her to get the point! I wanted her to think about how it felt to be Leona. So instead of pushing, which would have felt great, I yelled, "Stop! Stop and think! What if I called you bad names like you do to Leona?"

But Alice didn't want to stop or think. Instead she gave me a shove which sent me sprawling on the hard pavement. I felt the sting of sand and cement on my hands and legs.

"So there, Miss Smarty." Alice was standing over me, glaring, and ready to kick me back down if I tried to get up. My knee was bleeding and my elbow hurt.

All of a sudden someone yanked Alice away. It was the tough bus driver, with Francie right beside him. They must have come around the corner just in time to see Alice knock me down.

Francie ran up to me. "Charlotte, what happened? Are you okay?"

"Yeah, I *really* am," I told her, laughing a little because I was still on the ground with a bleeding knee and other scrapes and bruises. The bus driver grabbed my arm and helped me up. Then he shook his big hammy finger first at Alice, then at Miriam.

"Look here, you two. No one knocks kids down around my bus. And," he shook his finger at them again, "no one bullies the kids on my bus." Miriam and Alice looked at the ground. "You're walkers, aren't you?" They nodded. "Then get started," he gestured toward the sidewalk, and we all watched a very quiet Alice and Miriam slinking away with not a word to say for themselves.

"What happened, Charlotte? What happened?" Francie was wild with excitement.

I told her about sticking up for Leona and telling Alice not to pick on her anymore.

"Hurrah! Hurrah for you, Charlotte! You forgot to be shy!" Francie was jumping all over the place.

When Francie said that, about my not being shy, I realized that I felt proud. For once, maybe for the first time in my life, instead of acting like a scaredy cat, I had actually done something brave. I had *still* been afraid but even so, I had stood up against something I thought was wrong. Instead of just thinking that something was unfair, I did something about it!

I heard a tapping on the bus window and looked up. There was Leona clasping her hands over her head and shaking them together the way boxers do when they win. She was proud of me, too.

"*Ça va!*" I mouthed to her as the bus pulled out. "*Ça va!*"

Mary E. Finger grew up in a small town in New Hampshire during the Depression of the 1930s. She currently lives in Pawtucket, Rhode Island. This is her first novel for children.

Drawing has been a part of Kimberly Rose Batti's life for as long as she can remember. Her love of art led her to pursue a BFA in illustration at Rhode Island School of Design and an MFA at William Paterson University.

DATE DUE